THIS WARMER BOOK BELONGS TO:

_____   _____

_____   _____

_____   _____

_____   _____

First published 1999 by Walker Books Ltd
87 Vauxhall Walk, London SE11 5HJ

This edition published 2000

2 4 6 8 10 9 7 5 3 1

This book has been typeset in Stempel Schneidler.

Printed in Hong Kong

British Library Cataloguing in Publication Data
A catalogue record for this book is
available from the British Library.

ISBN 0-7445-7252-5

RABBIT FOOD

Susanna Gretz

WALKER BOOKS
AND SUBSIDIARIES
LONDON • BOSTON • SYDNEY

Celery, tomatoes, peas, carrots and
mushrooms – that's rabbit food!
Dickie and Debbie
love all of it.
John doesn't.
"Don't you want to grow up
big and strong?" asks his mum.

"**NO**," says John.
"Why not?" asks Dad.
"Because grown-ups eat celery and
tomatoes and peas and carrots," says John,
"and, worst of all, mushrooms…"

Yuk!

The truth is, John hardly eats any rabbit food at all.
"Maybe he's just not hungry enough," says Mum.
"Maybe Uncle Bunny can help," says Dad.

Dad makes a quick telephone call,
and the very next day …

Uncle Bunny arrives!
Everyone is glad
to see him.

"Now, we're off for the weekend," says Mum.
"Uncle Bunny will look after you."
"There's food in the kitchen," says Dad,
"and please see that John eats some of everything."

"Righty-ho," says Uncle Bunny.

At lunchtime John builds a bridge
with his celery, tomatoes and carrots.
"Eat up," says Uncle Bunny. "They're delicious!"
"Yuk," says John.
"Eat your rabbit food and you'll grow big and
strong like me," says Uncle Bunny.
But when no one is looking …

Uncle Bunny
hides his carrots
under his
napkin.

At supper John makes a cave with his toast and
he hides his peas and mushrooms underneath.
"Try some," says Uncle Bunny.
"Just one teeny tiny bite. They're good for you."
"Yuk!" says John.
"Eat your rabbit food and you'll grow big and
strong like me!" says Uncle Bunny.
But when no one is looking …

Uncle Bunny hides his carrots in the flowerpot.

Next
morning
they all
play
football …

then
bunnyjump …

then
tug-of-war.

They get quite hungry.
Everyone, even John, tucks into Sunday lunch.
It's baked potato rabbits: the eyes are peas,
the noses are mushrooms, the mouths are bits of tomato,
the whiskers are bits of celery and the ears are carrots …
that is, all except for Uncle Bunny's rabbit.
"Why doesn't **your** rabbit have ears,
Uncle Bunny?" asks John.

Uncle Bunny doesn't seem to hear. "Hurry up and eat," he says. "We're off to climb a mountain this afternoon!"

Debbie reaches the mountain top first.

That evening, everyone is **very** hungry.
Uncle Bunny puts what's left of the food on the table,
but first he wants to watch the News.
"Help yourselves,"
he tells the little rabbits.
John is so hungry,
he eats lots of everything.

Now Uncle Bunny wants some food, too.
But there's not a scrap left on the table.
All that's left in the kitchen is a bunch of carrots.
"You don't like carrots, do you, Uncle?" says John.

"Well, I, uh … **no**,"
says Uncle Bunny.

"But they're delicious!"
yells John, and everyone jumps
on Uncle Bunny.

"They're good for you!
Just *try* a little! Just one teeny tiny
bite … and you'll grow
BIG and **STRONG** like **US!**"

Uncle Bunny bites off
a very tiny bit of carrot.
He chews it very slowly.
Then he bites off another
tiny bit … and another.

Just then Mum and Dad appear.
"I did the best jump!" Dickie tells them.
"I climbed the mountain first!" says Debbie.
"I ate celery and tomatoes and carrots and peas," says John,
"and **MUSHROOMS!**"

Mum and Dad are delighted.
"However did you do it, Uncle Bunny?" says Dad.
"You're terrific," says Mum.
Uncle Bunny doesn't answer, for his mouth is full of carrots.

"In fact," he says at last, "they're not bad."